The

ALIEN'S

DAUGHTER

The Alien's Daughter

S&G Publishing, Knoxville, TN
www.sgpublish.com

Library of Congress Cataloging-in-Publication Data

Morrows, JC | Morrows, Macy

 Alien's Daughter, The / JC Morrows, Macy Morrows

1. Teen / Fiction / Aliens. 2. Teen / Fiction / Coming-of-Age. 3. Teen / Fiction / Family. 4. Teen / Fiction / Social Issues. 5. Teen / Fiction / Science Fiction and Fantasy

ISBN: 978-1948733991

2018937664

Cover and Internal Design © 2018 Expresso Designs
Cover Image by Expresso Designs

First Edition 2018

PRINTED AND BOUND IN THE UNITED STATES OF AMERICA

THE ALIEN'S DAUGHTER

TALES OF A TEENAGE ALIEN HUMAN HYBRID
BOOK ONE

JC MORROWS
WITH MACY MORROWS

S&G PUBLISHING

BOOKS BY JC MORROWS

ORDER OF THE MOONSTONE SERIES
A Reluctant Assassin
A Treacherous Decision
A Desperate Escape
A Tragic Consequence
A Broken Kingdom

SHORT STORIES AND NOVELLAS
A Perilous Assignment
A Cunning Masquerade
A Dangerous Love
A Covert Alliance
A Mysterious Masque

FROZEN WORLD SERIES
Life After E.L.E.
Escape After E.L.E.

WITH MACY MORROWS
TALES OF A TEENAGE ALIEN HUMAN HYBRID
THE ALIEN'S DAUGHTER
THE HYBRID CHALLENGE
(COMING SOON)

CONTENTS

For all of the girls out there who never felt like they really connected with their dad and didn't understand why.

You are NOT alone!

"A daughter should never have to beg her father for a relationship."

~ unknown

The Door With a Mind of its Own

So, today completely sucked.

Have you ever had one of those days? You know the one. . . where you keep thinking things couldn't get any worse, but then . . . they do?

Yeah, today was one of those days.

All day long, I tried to tell myself that it was just my imagination, that what I thought I was seeing. . . wasn't real. . . couldn't be real, that I could not really be seeing. . . what I thought I saw. When my bedroom door opened all by itself —for the third time—there was really no denying that something strange was going on.

"You saw that, right?"Kayla's voice was shaky, hesitant, less sure than I had ever heard it. And since she was the kind of girl who would befriend the biggest freak at Leighton Middle School, the type who would stare down the school bully and the head cheerleader without batting an eyelash, someone who would readily defend me. . . and anyone else who the popular crowd chose to target, that was really saying something.

Crap. Yeah, there was no denying it now—especially since Kayla was asking me if I had seen it.

If she saw it, and she's the most level-headed person I know, I'm not about to argue with her about whether or not I saw. . . what I thought I saw.

If she says she saw it. . . then she saw it. Even if I know it's impossible.

"Yeah, I saw it." I answered reluctantly, looking at the expression on Kayla's face. This was not how I wanted my summer to start.

Especially this summer.

"Weird, huh."

"Yeah. Weird." She kept watching the door.

Probably waiting to see if it does it again.

After several seemingly endless, edgy seconds, she went back to flipping through the magazine in her hand, but every few pages, she would look back over at the door.

Great. Just great. Crap. Crap. Crap! What is going on with me lately?

This wasn't the first thing to happen. There

had been more than a few odd things happening with me for the last few weeks. So many I hardly knew what to think.

There was the time I had been making popcorn and the microwave had gone nuts, popping so fast, the bag had pretty much exploded. And the last day of school had been insane.

My locker had done the same sort of weird thing, the door popping open without my even having to put in my combination—though I had chalked that up to old doors and rusty hinges. What else could it be. . . right?

Now there was this crazy door thing.

I kept looking at the stupid door, hoping it wouldn't do the same thing again.

Or at least find some logical explanation for what it's doing.

When I realized that I was watching my friend watch the door, I actually started to regret calling her.

But. . . since I was being shipped off to my dad's the very next day, it had seemed like a good idea to spend my last day of fun summer vacation with my best friend—really my only friend.

And then the door had started its' strange little dance.

Maybe our house is haunted.

I thought about one of Kayla's other friends who had come to school after Christmas break, telling stories about their Aunt's house.

I could still remember how everyone around the table had watched her as she told stories. They'd hung on her every word, as if she was revealing embarrassing secrets about the popular kids.

So, maybe that was the case with our house. . . maybe.

It could happen.

The more I thought about, the more appealing the idea became. *Yeah, I like that idea. If our house is haunted, I don't have to be any bigger a freak than I already am, right?* It could be such a cool, fun story to tell people.

Hey, our house is haunted. *Yeah, I mean. . . sure we've lived here for ten years and if it was going to happen, you'd think it would have happened way before now, but really that's the only logical explanation. . . right?*

Okay. . . so, maybe the house wasn't haunted.

But then, if the house is not haunted—and Kayla really saw my bedroom door open three times all by itself, with absolutely no other explanation that either one of us could come up with, then someone had to be doing it.

We would both have to agree that I'm not super fast, and Kayla's never shown any sign of telekinetic abilities that I knew of, and neither of us knew anyone who could turn invisible, so what could it be?

Truthfully, I don't want to know. I'm just glad Kayla didn't jump up and run out of my room after the third time—kinda like what I wanted to do, but didn't because if she can handle staying. . . I can stay, too.

But seriously, what is going on?

* * *

We never did figure it out. We talked about it for almost an hour, until Kayla said she had to go home for dinner, and neither of us had a clue what could make the door open by itself.

After she left, I didn't even bother to watch for a text from her. Whatever had been happening with that door, she'd obviously been freaked out, since she had said when she came over earlier that she would be staying for dinner if it was fine with my mom. . . and it was.

It always was—and Kayla knew that. Mom always made the comment that Kayla was welcome anytime, when we asked if she could come over or stay for dinner, or spend the night at our house—which was a lot.

I was usually grateful for Kayla's company, but this time I didn't argue. I had just nodded and told her I would talk to her later, thinking that I would need to figure out what was going on with the door before that call.

And I certainly hadn't told Kayla that all three

times the door opened—all by itself—I had just been thinking of how much I wished I could get out of here. . . out of my room, out of my house, to go any place that would keep me from having to spend two months with my father.

My father. . . the man who had confused me my whole life. The man who—half the time—I wasn't even sure liked me, much less loved me.

He spent time with me because the court had given it to him—and because my mom had a tendency to call him up and yell at him if he didn't take some of it at least every few months. Though why he had decided to take the two-month summer vacation time that he hadn't taken in five years. . . *the summer before I start high-school. . .* the summer that could actually be an opportunity to find some way to fit in with kids I would be going to high school with in the fall.

I had no idea.

But he had called Mom and told her that he would love to have me for the summer. She had been so excited, she'd made me an appointment for a makeover, then she had gone out and bought me a whole new wardrobe, just for the occasion. . . then we had done the whole spa thing, including a mani, pedi, styling, a little trim. . .

Tugging on a lock of my freakishly colored hair, I almost wished we had dyed it again.

Dad always looked at me like I was a freak when I showed up with my crazy weird blue hair. So much so, that when I was just five years old, Mom had gone out and bought me several wigs to wear, for the few times he had actually agreed to a visit.

By age ten, she had decided that it would be

safe enough to use a temporary color rinse whenever I was supposed to go visit him, which I had been very happy about because it made me feel normal for those few days.

I had even asked Mom if I could use something more permanent after that first weekend of feeling like I actually fit in with the world around me—instead of standing out so vividly. Her answer had been a firm and resounding *"No"* but I had kept hoping. . . and trying. . . to get her to change her mind.

It was only recently, when everywhere we went we saw someone with blue or purple or pink hair, that I had decided to stop fighting it and deal with my inexplicably blue hair.

And for the summer, with swimming in mind, crazy colored hair being popular for the first time in my life, and since the stylist had looked at us like we were nuts when we'd suggested changing the color, we had finally decided it might be best to just leave it.

But I was not looking forward to the look on Dad's face when he saw it. He always got this weird frown that made him look like he was about to bite a stick in half or something.

It wasn't very flattering—not one bit, but I had to admit that the stylist had a point.

If I spent any amount of time in the pool—or the ocean—depending on where Dad decided we would go for vacation, the color would either fade quickly or turn some ridiculously unflattering shade of green or orange or sickly puce.

So now I was going to visit my dad, with my blue hair and my annoyance over missing a whole summer at home with my mom and Kayla, who both actually enjoyed spending time with me. And to make matters worse, there was now this weird door thing to deal with.

It just wasn't fair.

"Zoe, are you all packed, sweetie?"

I sighed at the concern in my mother's voice. She knew I tended to drag my feet when it was time to get ready for a visit with my dad—and, while I appreciated that she wanted to make sure my time with Dad was no more strained than it absolutely had to be, it was a little frustrating that she knew me well enough to know that I was doing everything I could to find a way to delay my departure as much as I possibly could.

With a little huff, I answered as truthfully as I could. "I'm working on it" I answered, as I threw a shirt into the mostly empty suitcase that was open on my bed.

Picking up the sundress with skinny little

straps and turning it over in my hands, I debated whether or not to pack it. I still remembered Mom laughing when she pulled the hanger off the rack. "Since we decided to leave your hair alone, I think you should try this one."

She had been kidding, but I had taken her to heart, taking it and laying it over my arm with the rest of the clothes she had picked out. "Great idea, Mom."

I had laughed and moved on to the next rack —while she stood there with a surprised look on her face for several minutes, before coming over to where I stood, randomly pulling tee-shirts off the rack in front of me.

And though she had only been kidding. . . and I had only taken it thinking that it would drive Dad nuts, wearing something that would make my hair stand out even more than it did with no help whatsoever. . . when I had tried it on later in the dressing room, we had both been forced to admit that it really was a great choice.

The dress made me feel—and look—more grown up than I felt most of the time. It was just funky enough to be cute, while maintaining a sense of maturity that most clothes that fit me could never achieve. My mind made up, I tossed it in after the shirt. . . just as Mom walked through the doorway of my room.

"You and I have a very different idea of what *all packed* means, Zoe."

"I didn't say I was all packed." I grinned mischievously at her. "I said I was working on it. I am."

"Well, this is not what I meant when I told you to pack before your dad actually pulls into the driveway, Zo."

My shoulders drooped at the disappointment in her voice.

She was right—and I knew it. I had a bad habit of waiting until Dad's rental car pulled into the driveway before I actually forced myself to throw a few things into a suitcase.

"You're spending two months with him, Zo— and you're flying out tomorrow evening. You know as well as I do that it is a bad idea to make him wait. You have to be ready to go as soon as he gets here."

"I know, Mom. I'm sorry." I wanted to rebel. I wanted to find some way to make him so mad, he would leave without me, but I didn't want to upset Mom any more than I had already.

Only one other time had I made him wait long enough that he'd decided to just let me stay home—and since he had fussed at Mom pretty much the whole time he had been waiting for me, it totally was not worth it.

So I blew out a breath, squared my shoulders and got serious about packing.

Not Exactly What I was Expecting.

"We're going where? Seriously?"

When Mom handed me the plane ticket that had arrived by special messenger weeks ago, I hadn't paid any attention to the destination

But now I couldn't take my eyes off the little black line of text that told me this summer vacation might just be better than I'd hoped.

Hawaii.

"I can hardly believe it. I mean, Dad hates tropical destinations."

"Well, maybe he wants this summer to be special." Mom smiled as she answered. It was obvious she thought she had landed on the right answer and she'd completely forgotten about the fact that Dad never did anything he didn't want to do. . . unless he did.

Truly he was the most confusing person I had ever met. One visit with him, we would go hiking and horseback riding, on picnics and swimming excursions. The next time, I would end up hiding out in the clubhouse while he golfed and hung out with his weird friends.

I never knew what to expect from him. Sometimes I almost wondered if he was secretly two different people. . . or if he was actually a set of twins who just randomly switched lives, and I only ended up with the cool one every third or fourth visit.

Of course, Mom had nixed both theories. Plus, a quick search on the Internet had revealed that he didn't have a twin, or an evil doppelganger, at least as far as I could find any evidence for. . . or rather the lack of any.

So, I would just have to live with the Dad I had—the one who had married my mom after some crazy whirlwind weekend, where they had met and then gotten married less than twenty-four hours later. Of course, he was also the one who had decided he didn't want to be married to Mom anymore when I was just six months old, and he was also the one who only wanted me some of the time. . . like when Mom made him visit.

This was my life.

Though it didn't feel like it at the moment,

for the most part, my life was pretty great. There were just a few exceptions, like when my crazy dad decided he wanted to take the summer vacation he had never wanted. . . on a whim.

Oh well, at least I'll have the beach to make it a little better this year.

"Zo, sweetheart. . ." Mom's questioning tone got my attention.

"Yeah, Mom?"

"If you didn't know where you were going, are you sure you packed everything you're going to need?"

"Oh, crap." Panicked, I ran towards my room. With such a great destination ahead of me, I didn't want to do anything now that might cause Dad to decide not to take me. I would have to repack. . . and fast!

I dumped both suitcases on my bed, shaking

loose the last few things that stubbornly clung to the inside and running a hand over the pile to spread everything out, pulling things from both piles that I would definitely not need on a beach.

Thirty seconds later, I had a stack of clothes that would need to go back in my drawers and closet—and only enough clothes to fill one suitcase.

Definitely not enough for two whole months.

I spent the next twenty minutes rushing around my room, putting clothes away, pulling new items out, stacking them on my bed, then running back to the drawers to pull out a few things I had put away when it occurred to me that maybe we wouldn't be spending the entire two months at the beach.

Pants and socks, long-sleeved shirts and a light jacket I had just returned to my closet went on the pile again. I dug my hiking boots back out from under the bed and went searching for the bag that kept the rest of my clothes safe from being mauled by the rough soles.

"How's it going?"

I mumbled something in return as I pushed myself further under the bed, trying to reach the elusive bag that I must have knocked to the other side earlier when I'd tossed my boots under the bed.

"Aha! Got it!" I shimmied back out and popped to my feet, stuffing the boots inside before the bag somehow ran off again.

"Oh, good. I was worried you would just dump half the clothes out and end up with nothing you could wear somewhere other than the beach."

She sounded so proud of me, I ducked my

head, keeping quiet about the fact that I had indeed done just that before I thought about it.

"Need any help?" She asked, picking up one of my thinner long-sleeved shirts and folding it before placing it inside the nearest suitcase.

"Actually, I do." I held up the skimpy swimsuit Mom had bought me on our shopping trip—one I was certain I would never get up enough nerve to wear. "Do you know where my other suit is?"

The one I like way better, the one that actually covers all of me, the one I'm comfortable wearing. . .

She nodded, but said nothing.

After a few seconds of silence, I pressed. "Mom, do you know where it is?"

"I do, but it won't help you."

"Anna borrowed it, didn't she?"

I would never understand why my mother's diminutive sister felt as if my wardrobe was available to her whenever she liked.

"And she said she would have it back in time, didn't she?"

Mom nodded again, her eyes trained on the shirt she was folding.

"But it's not here, so she didn't bring it back at all, did she?"

"I'm certain your father can take you shopping for another if you feel you need to."

I suppressed the urge to say something that I knew would only get me in trouble, trying to reason out why Mom always stuck up for her troublesome sister.

Aunt Anna only showed up to visit if she wanted something. Most of the time it was money that she just expected Mom to supply, but too often those visits coincided with a raid of my sparse, but expensive wardrobe.

At least the trust that Dad had set up for me would pay for the loss of the swimsuit, though it would certainly not guarantee that I could find another one that was as perfect for me as it had been.

It was difficult enough shopping for clothes to go with a ridiculous body and blue hair. *But then to have to replace the stuff she steals all the time.*

It was enough to have me stomping across the room and throwing the next few items into the suitcase. . . without folding a single thing.

I did not want to shop with Dad. It was always a fiasco.

He had no patience with me even when there was no shopping involved. But put him in a store or a mall, surrounded by other teenage girls carrying bags of things he sneeringly referred to as junk. . . and it was a recipe for disaster.

"How long until he gets here? Is there any chance. . ."

But she cut me off. Mom always seemed to know what I was going to say. "There's no time, Zoe. Even if you were packed and ready to go, there's no way we could get there, find something that works, and get back here in time."

I stomped to my closet again, pulling out my absolute least favorite swimsuit from two summers ago, praying that I wouldn't need it—and hoping that it would still fit—as I practically flung it into the second suitcase.

"I am sorry, Zo. You know she never means to take your stuff and not bring it back."

I nodded as I stomped over to the closet again, rummaging through outfits I had already looked at and discarded as possibilities. I knew she didn't technically mean to, and I knew she was family, and I knew I could replace the stuff she never returned, but it didn't make me feel any better about the fact that she always did it—and she always got away with it.

Just one more way I get the short end of the stick.

For the Record, I Hate Airplanes

Despite our best efforts. . .

When Dad arrived, I was not ready to go.

"He's here, Zoe. Are you ready?" Mom's voice floated up the stairs to me, where I was busily trying to stuff the last few things I would need into my carry-on bag.

"Yes, Mom. I'm coming!" I yelled down, as I hefted the heavy suitcases off my bed.

"Do you need some help with those, Zoe?" The sound of my father's voice startled me. It was bright and filled with happiness.

I turned to look at the man I was never quite convinced I shared blood with.

It was no surprise that he and my mom had gotten together. She was gorgeous and he was what my friends would call movie-star handsome. *Just one more reason I'm sure I was adopted. . . or maybe switched at birth.*

Gorgeous—I was not.

He was tall and well-built, even though as far as I knew, he lived off his own trust fund and he played golf—nothing else. He sported a natural tan. *That would be one perk of playing golf all the time.* And he had this one streak of silver hair that looked as if it was on purpose, something he paid a salon to create for him. . . to make him look distinguished.

Not a blue hair anywhere. I waited for the look, or a comment about my hair, but none came.

Instead, he righted the bags I had knocked to the floor in my hurry, slipped my carry-on over his shoulder, and smiled. "You ready, sweet pea?"

I nodded. *Looks like I'm getting the Dad who likes me.*

The summer was definitely looking up.

He hadn't looked at me like I was a freak for having blue hair. He was helping me with my heavy bags—and not fussing about my not being ready on time. And in a couple of hours, we would be heading to the beach.

"My goodness. Have you got all of that, David?" Mom had apparently come up the stairs behind Dad and was reaching for a bag. . . though Dad wasn't letting her take anything. He carried the bags down the stairs like they weighed nothing, which I knew wasn't true since I had just packed them.

"No, I've got it Lara." He continued down the stairs, maneuvering the narrow steps surprisingly easily while carrying two large suitcases.

"Okay. If you're sure." She turned back to look at me, surprise all over her delicate features. I turned back to my bed, grabbing up the last few things I needed to stuff in my carry-on. After a minute, Mom and I followed Dad down the stairs and into the great room at the front of the house.

"Is that everything?" He turned back to me with a smile, and I nodded mutely.

I was so not used to the nice Dad.

"Okay, then. I'll just put these in the car."

As soon as he stepped outside, I turned to hug Mom. Nice Dad or not, I was going to miss my mom. Before now, the longest visit I had ever had with Dad had been about three weeks.

"Sweetheart, you're going to have so much fun."

"I know, but I'm going to miss you."

She held me tightly. "I'm going to miss you, too. You just don't know how much." She stepped back, but didn't let go completely. "Oh, it's going to be so quiet around here without you." Then she pulled me in for another hug. "But you are going to have fun."

I sighed heavily. "I know I will, especially since Dad actually seems happy to see me."

She let go again and stepped back a little, keeping a loose hold of my hand. "He does seem particularly happy, doesn't he?"

She looked out to where he was loading my suitcases into the large trunk of the car he had rented. I could see an emotion there that I did not see very often.

Mom was always very careful when she talked about Dad and their relationship. I could see for myself the times that he was mean to her or when he fussed for no good reason, but she always had good things to say about him, reminding me that he was my father and deserved my respect—if for no other reason.

I wasn't always so sure about it, but I never argued with her about it.

And every once in a while, especially when Nice Dad showed up, I would get to see how she still felt about him, but I was never really sure how I felt about it all.

If he was Nice Dad all the time, it might be different, but he wasn't—and I didn't want Mom to get hurt any more.

"Text me. . . a lot."

Before I could answer her, she added, "and have fun."

"I will." I answered with a laugh, hoping she would take the one answer for both of her prompts.

*   *   *

The airport was a bustling beehive of activity.

Probably lots of families heading off on vacation. The thought was not nearly as sour as it would have been. I was surprised to realize I was actually really looking forward to the trip ahead of us.

Well, except for the plane ride.

I hate airplanes.

It always took forever to get checked in and

through security, even flying first class. At least the first class lounge was nice, a lot nicer than others I had been in the other times I had flown somewhere with Dad.

Dad never flew anything but first class. Me, on the other hand, he sometimes sent to business class or economy plus. . . which was a small step up from coach.

This time, like the few other times he had actually flown out to meet me, we were both in first class. We were even seated next to each other, which I had not expected. I was certainly old enough to fly on my own by now.

Not that I mind. . . given that it's Nice Dad who showed up for this trip.

Once we found a comfy spot in the lounge to wait, he started peppering me with questions. What was new with me? Was I excited about school starting in the fall? Was there anyone special in my life?

I nearly spit out my soda at that question.

He looked at me with genuine shock. . . at least, after he finished patting me on the back and making sure I wasn't choking.

"Why do I get the feeling that you think that's a silly question?"

When I said nothing in return, he added, "You are a beautiful young woman. You should have someone special in your life." Then, after a dramatic pause, he continued.

"You're old enough for it now. . . right?" He ended on a note of uncertainty and I reminded myself that he had barely spent any time with me over the last few years—when things had gotten more and more difficult school-wise.

He would have no idea just how mean middle

school kids could be.

Especially if you happen to have a weird body and blue hair.

Not that I could really explain it all anyway, since I didn't understand it any better than he did.

We sat in strained silence for several minutes. When he started asking questions again, they were decidedly less personal.

Thank goodness.

I answered as honestly as possible and prayed the plane would be ready soon and we could board. . . and be on our way to Hawaii.

Ground Control to Major Mess-up.

I know I'm not the best flyer but there has to be some responsibility for that which rests with the pilot of the plane, doesn't there?

I mean, they're the ones who are guiding the plane through the air and the clouds. They should have some control over how rough or smooth the flight is. . . shouldn't they?

I know all about turbulence—and that's not at all what I mean when I say a rough or a smooth ride. *Not that I understand why a pilot wouldn't just take the plane higher or lower. . . away from the turbulence. . . when there is turbulence. They know all about it and everything.*

But then, I'm not a pilot so what do I know.

However, in the last ten years of my life, I have flown a number of times; first with my mom, who would fly out with me to meet Dad, then take a little vacation of her own once she had dropped me off. . . then by myself many times. . . and now with Dad.

So it's not like I don't have experience with all sorts of airplanes.

Of course, none of these experiences have been what I would call highly successful. Each one came with its own problems and glitches. Somehow. . .

something always seemed to go wrong—on every single flight I was ever on.

And that might account for at least a part of my having a problem with the whole experience.

Mom always said there was no reason to be nervous about flying. More people died in cars accidents than in plane crashes.

I never bothered to argue with her and tell her my problem wasn't about the safety of the plane, it was about the plane ride itself.

I was never nervous that we were going to crash. I just hated to fly. There was just something about hanging in midair in a steel tube with hundreds of other people that gave me the creeps.

And for some reason that I couldn't figure out, this trip was exceptionally rough. From checking in. . . to boarding the plane, several things went wrong—inexplicably wrong.

Oddly enough, each time, I was reminded of the weird stuff that had been happening all week. I kept telling myself that it couldn't possibly have anything to do with me. . . that I could be doing it. . . *or could I?*

Of course, that just made me think about my bedroom door unexpectedly opening—three times. I had tried to convince myself that I had not been doing that either.

I mean, how could I have been?

It still made no sense. How could I have been making the door open. . . from across the room? I couldn't. Really.

Right?

Except that Kayla had looked at me like she thought I had something to do with it—which I guess made sense in a weird way.

After all, it was my door, my room, and my weirdness.

But there was nothing I could think of that I was doing. . . or trying to do. . . to delay the flight.

I tried distracting myself by texting Mom. I even checked some of the silly social media accounts that Kayla had made me set up at the end of school.

I fidgeted and told myself to stop doing whatever it was I might be doing, but nothing seemed to make a bit of difference.

The first glitch, if you could call it that, was our reservation. The flight attendant who checked us in couldn't find anything in the computer that showed us actually checking in—and even though we had our tickets and our boarding passes, they almost didn't let us on the plane.

I'm still not sure how Dad managed it. But

somehow we weren't getting on. . . and then we were.

Next, our takeoff was delayed. . . and then nearly canceled when there was a problem on the runway. *And I know there was no way Dad could have done anything about that one.*

But somehow I got the impression that he did actually have something to with us finally getting clearance to take off on a different runway—though it never made any sense to me how he could have done anything about it.

Or maybe it was me. . . somehow. And wouldn't that be a good thing?

I mean. . . it wasn't like I was trying to do anything weird on the flight.

But then, I wasn't really trying to do anything with the door, even though it was kinda doing what I secretly wanted it to do at the time.

The real question now was how to get it to stop. Fast.

It was bad enough that Dad *(and everyone at school)* thought I was some sort of freak—well, Not Nice Dad, anyway.

If I was doing something, without meaning to, I had to figure out a way to stop.

But first I would have to figure out how I was doing whatever it was I was doing, which was no easy thing.

It wasn't like there was a button I could push or a switch I could flip. It wasn't like tying my shoes or writing my name. There was nothing in my head that told me I was doing it, so there was no way for me to figure out how to stop.

So I tried to make myself calm down instead, hoping that would help, even if nothing else did.

No such luck.

Our takeoff was exceptionally rough, *but that's really all I remember about it.* I must have been concentrating so hard on not throwing up or freaking out, that I blocked out everything else until the plane was actually in the air.

I do remember Dad reaching over at one point and telling me that I needed to calm down. He put a hand over mine and just left it there. He didn't squeeze and he didn't fuss. He just left his hand resting lightly on top of mine all through takeoff.

I'm not even sure when he lifted his hand—but at one point it was there. . . and then it was gone, and when I looked over at him, he was just sitting there, smiling. It was an odd smile, not mean or angry or even mischievous, but as if I had just let him in on some big secret—one that he was positively delighted by.

He watched me for several minutes without saying anything, just watching me and smiling.

I wanted to ask him what he was smiling about, but when I opened my mouth, I realized I didn't really want to know.

Maybe it's better to just leave it alone.

I was nervous enough just being on the plane. I certainly didn't want to ask any questions that could potentially start a conversation that might make me even more nervous.

*   *   *

Fortunately, the flight was relatively uneventful. . . almost boring. I even dozed off at some point, which was a relief. I had not been looking forward to the long flight. We were going cross-country, from Ohio to Hawaii. It would be a long flight.

But at least it's nonstop.

I didn't even want to think about how I would handle getting off one plane and then onto another. One was bad enough.

Sleeping through the long flight was truly a blessing to my battered nerves—though the massive headache I woke up with. . . was not so good.

It was the sort of pain that feels as if there is a stampede in your head. Every sound, every light, every movement felt as if my head would would split open any moment.

In other words, it was pure agony.

And there was no explanation for it. I had woken up in a normal position, not some weird contortionist position where my ear was touching my shoulder or my chin was on my chest. There was absolutely no reason for my head to feel as if a little gang of elves were digging for gold. . . with enormous pickaxes.

It was all I could do to get off the plane.

You Can't Ignore Me Forever.

Between the airport and the hotel, I really thought my head might just explode.

Fortunately, Dad must have seen that I was not doing well, because he had me lean on him all the way off the plane. Once we were in the terminal, he led me to a plush chair in the first-class lounge.

I took a moment to text Mom and tell her

we'd arrived before shoving the phone deep down into my bag, not wanting the bright screen anywhere near me, since light seemed to make my headache even worse, if that was possible.

Dad left to get me a drink—a soda—which he said should help a bit with my headache.

Did I tell him I had a headache? I didn't remember telling him about it, but he knew, and I didn't have the energy to worry about how.

I just wanted the pain to stop.

Somehow, we made it through the airport, with me leaning heavily against Dad, then we followed the signs to where our luggage was ready to be picked up and then made our way slowly toward the exit.

The pain never got any better, even though Dad had assured me that the soda would help.

I still didn't remember telling him I had a

headache.

Maybe he looked at my face and my obvious 'I'm in serious pain' body language and figured it out. Whichever way it was, I wasn't arguing or questioning it.

And for once, I was grateful for Dad's extravagant lifestyle choices.

We were picked up just outside the doors of the terminal—not the main door where a horde of greeters waited to shower you with flowers and loud tropical music played during what was essentially a huge welcome party.

Later I might wish I had experienced some of that, but at the moment, I was much too preoccupied with the intense pain in my head.

Dad left me again, but only long enough to go and retrieve our luggage and help the driver load it into the car's enormous trunk.

The ride to the hotel was mercifully a quiet one.

Dad handed me a moist, warm towel when he settled himself beside me in the back of the car and I gratefully leaned back against the seat and positioned it over my eyes.

Again I thought that I might wish later that I had seen some of the sights on the long drive to our hotel, but I comforted myself with the reminder that we would see it all again on our way back to the airport.

Not to mention the time we will have on the island.

I was tempted to ask Dad how long we would be here, but I couldn't bear the thought of dealing with the sound that would make in the nice, quiet car that was gliding through the streets with very little jostling of its passengers.

I would likely never know if the ride only felt like it lasted forever. . . or if the driver had been driving slower than usual so as not to aggravate my headache any more than necessary, but whichever one it was, I was grateful.

Dad was also kind enough not to do a lot of talking while we drove.

He asked me once if there was anything he could get for me. I quickly said no, snapping my mouth shut before the urge to be sick got too strong to avoid.

He also spoke to the driver once to confirm the name of our hotel. I kept any comments to myself, reluctantly acknowledging that it was more than a little important that we actually get to the right hotel.

When we finally reached the hotel, Dad opened his door to get out. I groaned at the crazy amount of bright sunshine that had invaded the dark car and slumped down in the seat, paying no attention whatsoever to the hotel. . . just the pain that still held me prisoner.

He quickly slipped out with barely a sound, shutting out the bright light. I was more than happy to stay in the dark, quiet car until he came back and I would have to deal with noise and light.

Fortunately, the driver turned into an underground parking structure, an enclosed one that was nice and dark, where Dad met us and together he and the driver got our things unloaded.

We took the elevator up to our floor. I glanced around and noticed how bright the lights were in the hall and the elevator, even though I had left my sunglasses on. I quickly shut my eyes again.

At one of the floors where the elevator stopped, someone must have given us an odd look because I heard Dad whisper a little too loudly, "headache" but no one else said anything.

I tried looking around when we got off the elevator at our floor because I knew Dad would expect me to say something about the hotel later, but even the lights on our floor—lowered to a discreet dimness—were too much for me and I resigned myself to either saying nothing. . . or lying.

*   *   *

We had taken no more than a step inside the door when Dad set down the bags and turned to me.

"Sweetheart, you've dealt with that pain long enough. Let me help."

I went slowly, but willingly, curious as to what he thought he could do to alleviate what could only be a migraine of the worst sort.

"I am truly sorry for this, but temporarily knocking you out was necessary."

His words got my attention—as did the sudden decrease of pain I quickly noted when he took my hand.

"I'm sorry. What? You did what?"

"I put you out. . . and I am sorry for the after-effects. I know the headache was no picnic, but it really was necessary. You could have crashed the plane. That would have given both of us away—and killed hundreds of innocents."

Crashed the plane?

Put me out?

What is he talking about!

I shook my head, trying to figure out if I was

hearing things. . .

"I don't understand."

And I mean I really don't understand.

"Once I realized you were subconsciously sabotaging everything, I was able to override what you were doing and put you into a deep sleep until we landed." He patted my hand gently and smiled.

"A deep sleep. . . how? I mean, really, how did you do something like that?"

"I can explain everything, but first you need tell me you believe me when I say it was necessary, Zoe."

When I continued to glare at him, he added. "It was for your safety as well as everyone else's on the plane."His tone was almost ridiculously calm.

Is he saying what I think he's saying?

"Are you—"I stopped, then tried again a second later.

"Do you mean to say that I. . . that you think. . . wait, what exactly are you saying?"

"I am saying that your burgeoning abilities were overwhelming you in a high-stress situation and it was necessary for me to take steps to ensure the safety of you and everyone else on board the plane."

"Yeah, that's what I thought you said." I knew my voice sounded flippant, but I was seriously trying to figure out if he was crazy.

Or if I was. . .

Because it really felt like it could be me. I was freaking out so much inside that I didn't know what to say. . . or think. . . about any of it.

And there was absolutely nothing in his voice that told me he was even remotely freaking out. . .

which might have actually been part of why I was freaking out so much.

"Why are you not shocked about all of this!"

His blind acceptance was too much for me to handle. . .

I Knew it. I Really am a Freak.

You know those moments. . .

The ones that blindside you and make you start to wonder if you're crazy. . . I mean really crazy, like locked up in a padded room with a fancy white jacket that wraps you up and keeps you from hurting yourself or anyone else. . .

Yeah . . . *that's where I am right now. And I wish I was kidding.* Not to mention, I couldn't figure out why Dad was so calm about the whole thing.

He should have been as freaked out about all this as I was. . . shouldn't he? But he wasn't. Instead, he was outrageously calm about it all.

And watching him sitting on the couch across from me, looking relaxed instead of freaked out, it finally occurred to me why he was so calm.

"You knew!" I yelled the words, not caring for the moment that I was talking to my father and that I should be speaking with more respect. Shock won out over common-sense.

"You knew about this all along, didn't you!"

He was still smiling, but he shook his head before he answered. "I did not know, or at least, I was not absolutely certain. This type of thing is not exactly commonplace among my people." He stood up and walked over to the sliding glass door that led outside.

I started to ask what he meant by *his people,* but snapped my lips shut before I could say the words.

I really. . . really, really. . . didn't want to know what he meant by that.

"Zoe, honey, you must have suspected. . . at least a little over the years." He walked over to me, took my hands in his.

And when he did, my headache was gone. . . all at once, just gone. . . not in a way like it got better, but as if it had never been there at all.

It almost distracted me from what he was saying. . . almost.

"I mean, sweetheart, you've got blue hair."

The first words out of my mouth were not exactly what I meant to say. "You hate my blue hair. Usually, you look at me like I'm the biggest freak in the universe when I leave it blue."

His smile disappeared initially, but somewhere in the middle of my outburst, it came back—then it got bigger.

I didn't want to think about why. I didn't want to know what I had said to make him smile like that, but he cleared his throat a little and started talking again.

"Not all the time though. . . right?"

He looked at me—and I looked at him, and he just kept holding my hands and looking as if he was expecting me to say something.

"What do you mean?" I blurted the words out, not even sure myself of the reason why.

"I know there have been times when it seemed like I did not like your hair, but there were also times when I had no problem with it at all."

"So what. . ." I shrugged, trying to brush off the suggestion he as making.

"Nevertheless, you were the one who decided it would be better to cover it up or change the color. I never wanted that."

I started to argue, but he stopped me.

"Okay. Maybe you thought that was what I wanted. Maybe I even said at some point that was what I wanted, but I didn't." He stopped, held up his hands in the universal gesture for 'I just don't know' and then went on.

"Well, *I didn't anyway.*" He stopped again, took a breath, and started again.

"I am not explaining this right. I honestly never expected to have the chance to tell you about all of this so I didn't take time to think it through."

I just stood there, shaking my head, trying to

figure out what he was talking about.

"I mean, I just thought when you didn't show any signs as a newborn. . ." He shrugged before going on.

"Of course, then the blue hair. . . and your figure of course. . . But I concluded that was it. I believed the human part just cancelled out most of the other. How could I have known it would take this long to show up?"

He looked like he was talking to himself more than me at this point—or at least, I wasn't having any luck following his weird, one-sided conversation.

"This did just start, right? Or has it been happening for a while now and I didn't know?"

He turned, taking my hands in his again and looking at me with an intense, searching expression—like he was looking for some outward sign of whatever he was talking about.

When he didn't say anything for a minute, I realized he was waiting for me to answer.

I struggled to figure out what the question had been.

"Zoe, honey?" He spoke gently, but gave me no clue as to what I was supposed to answer.

"Yeah?" I hoped he would take my clueless expression as prompting enough to know that I had no idea how to answer. . . or what to say.

"Zoe, when did all of this start, honey?"

"When did all of what start?"

"When did you start exhibiting abilities?" He asked the question like it was obvious—and I felt super slow for missing it.

"Abilities. . . that's what this is?"

"Well, yes." Again, he sounded like it was obvious—and I was just missing it.

"I'm pretty sure whatever it is—it just started." I answered slowly, thinking of the door again.

Had I been doing it?

Really?

Oh man!

I am a freak.

The thought made me want to run, hide, find a hole in a mountain—no, under a mountain—and never come out.

I had been doing it. I had made the door open by itself. . . three times. And apparently I had done something to the computers at the airport, and something to the plane. He had stated that I would have made the plane crash.

Would we have survived if the plane had crashed?

If that was the case, why had my head been

hurting so much? If I was going to have some stupid abilities, shouldn't that mean I wouldn't get headaches anymore. . . or stomachaches. . . or allergies.

"What exactly is it that started?" I asked the question slowly—still not entirely sure I wanted to know the answer.

"Your abilities are emerging." His smile was about as wide as I had ever seen it—and so bright, it literally could have lit up the room around us.

Absently, I wondered if that was somehow one of his abilities.

I mean, he has to have them, right? Otherwise, how would he know about them? Logically, that had to be the answer. He knows about the abilities, so he must have them too.

Mom had never said anything about any abilities. Did she know but had never told me about them? Wait. . . did she even know?

"What exactly. . ." I stumbled a little, but kept going, trying to get the question out. "I mean, how do you know about all this? And why didn't you ever say anything to me before? What exactly are you? What am I?"

He smiled again, before answering.

"You are half alien."

No Way. Not in This Lifetime.

I could not have heard him right, Could I? Had I? I mean. . . *did he really just say that I was half alien?*

"Well, actually I guess it might be more like a quarter. I'm not a biologist so I really have no idea how that part works."

He stopped to take a breath. I would have asked a question. . . if I had been able to form the words, but he went on without giving me the chance to pull my thoughts together enough to speak.

"However it works, this body is part human. I mean he walks around as a human whenever I am not here. And I have to tell you, I will do whatever I can to make sure that I am here more often now. For one thing, you are going to need help."

Help? Help with what? I did not like the sound of that. I tried again to speak. . . to ask what he meant by that, but my mouth—or my brain—still wasn't working.

"Anyway, whatever the percentage is, you are part alien. . . obviously."

"Obviously." I muttered.

He didn't seem to notice. He went right on talking while he walked all around the room.

"I never expected this. I mean, I did, but then, when you. . ." He gestured to me as if it somehow explained everything. "Well, when you were so obviously human, I did not think much about it."

"Is that why you left us?" I said the words quietly—and they were somewhat of a surprise even to me. I hadn't really meant to ask that—but of course, the question had always been there.

He rushed back over to me, kneeling in front of the chair I had dropped down onto.

"No, honey. It was not like that. Not at all. I was crazy in love with you the moment I saw you. It didn't matter to me if you were all human—or not."

"Then why did you leave?"

"Well, I didn't. I mean, I did, but not like you mean."

I started to ask what he meant again, but he stopped me.

"What I mean is, the human is the one who left you and your mother here on Earth. I did leave, in a way. I had to go back to my planet. I can only maintain the connection for so long and I was supposed to come back sooner than I was able, but there were some complications and I missed a couple of windows."

I started to interrupt again, but he quickly went on.

"The point is, I was too late to stop the human from leaving you and your mother. I tried to find a way to fix it, but. . ." He stopped then, letting go of my hands and moving away to pace back and forth across the room, obviously restless.

After a minute, he spoke again, though he stayed where he was, his back to me. "I would have done anything to come back here and be with the two of you, but the damage was already done and I did not have permission to reveal the truth about myself to your mother."

"So, Mom doesn't even know?"

He turned then, only shaking his head at first in answer. When he finally spoke, his voice was filled with emotion. "Perhaps if I had disobeyed and told her, even without permission, things would be different now."

I only sat there, watching him, uncertain of what I could—or should—say.

A moment ago, I had been angry with him. I had wanted to scream at him, certain that he had deserted Mom and me because I had not been what he'd been expecting, but the truth of it was nothing like I imagined.

None of this is what I expected. How could

I? Thoughts were rushing around in my head, falling all over each other and making me dizzy. *How could anyone see any of this craziness coming?*

Somehow all of the resentment and anger that had built up within me over the years was gone, replaced by uncertainty—and pity.

I could never have thought to feel sorry for him—for losing us. How could I have even known to feel for him?

This whole half human. . . half alien. . . thing is very confusing.

"So, wait. . ." I waited until he turned to look at me before going on.

"You say you left. Does that mean you went back to your planet? And what exactly do you mean by connection? Are you sharing the body physically or psychically or what?"

He actually smiled a little.

"It is actually both. When this body was chosen for me, he was taken from the planet. . ." He laughed before adding, "what you would call an alien abduction."

I shook my head as he laughed. *So not funny.* It was too weird to think of the man I had always known as my father—only being part of the man who had given me life.

"He was taken into a special environment on my ship and a part of my body was blended with his so that we are able to link."

He waved a hand in the air dismissively. "I will not go into the entire procedure. It is boring and I do not even understand some of the complexities. I am not a healer."

"I'm good with that." I insisted. " So, he has some of your body?"

"My code. . . well, DNA would be a more accurate term—or at least one that you would understand." He looked to me questioningly and I nodded to show him I did indeed understand.

"Once our bodies were compatible, the link was established and he was returned to Earth. . . to his home."

"And when you link, what happens to him?" Now I was trying not to panic at the thought of my father evicting someone from his own body.

"He is still there—and on some level, he knows what is going on."

He stopped a moment, walking back towards the window. "At times, I do have to create false memories for him, but that is a rarity."

"So, if he remembers marrying my mother, and. . . me. . . being his daughter, why doesn't he. . ." I couldn't finish. It was too weird to think that the Dad I had known all these years, the one who apparently didn't like me, was actually my human father, and the one who did like me was an alien.

It was just too weird.

But apparently he got enough of my meaning to answer my unspoken question. "I have often wondered about that myself. On the home world there is no emotion. And when I first met your mother, I was certain it was the human emotions and weakness of flesh that made our attachment so strong."

I looked down at my feet, blushing at the depth of emotion in his voice.

I really hope he doesn't start talking about their physical relationship. I don't want to think about Mom having sex—with a human or an alien.

"Even after he left the two of you, I couldn't be certain. Had I been affected by the connection to him—or somehow affected by the intense connection to his human body?"

I looked up when he stopped. He didn't say anything else for about a minute or two.

"So, you thought you were under the influence of his emotions? Why did you even come back?"

He turned to face me before answering the question. "Because I couldn't bear to stay away. I love the two of you too much—for whatever reason—and I do not want to be without you."

"Then why don't you come around more often?" I was starting to feel a little of the anger coming back now. He loved us. He wanted us. But he clearly hadn't been around very much, because I had spent too many tense weekends with Not

Nice Dad to think otherwise.

" I'm sorry. I'm afraid I don't have a good reason, at least not one you would consider to be a good reason."

"That's crap." I stood, fists clenched hard at my sides, a strange feeling running over my skin, a strange red at the edge of my vision."

He stepped forward quickly. "Zoe, you must listen to me. You must calm yourself. These abilities will control you if you allow them to. You must not let that happen."

I heard his voice. I understood the words, but it felt as if there were two forces at war inside of me and they were threatening to rip me in two.

One wanted to punish the Dad in front of me for leaving me. The other only wanted me to calm down.

The forces were strong; for what felt like an

eternity I could only deal with the internal battle that was raging. . . the anger and the calm.

Idly, I found myself wondering which one would win. And what would that mean for my Dad. . . and for me?

When I could see exactly what it would mean, especially if the side that wanted punishment won, common sense took hold of me. I did not want that.

"That is the alien within. We are a very impulsive people. . . much too quick to act instinctively. Far too often it has been our downfall."

I jumped back at the words that sounded in my head, responding the same way without even realizing I was doing it.

"Was that you? Were you speaking to me—in my head?"

"It is, yes. I did not think you would hear me if I spoke aloud."

I realized then that there was a lot of noise in the room around us. Nearly everything in the room was flying around us in a giant vortex of wind and sound.

"WOW! Am I doing that? How do I stop it?"

The moment I thought of stopping, everything around me stopped, right where it was and just. . . hovered in the air around the two of us.

"Did you?"

He was shaking his head. "No, that was you. Very good."

They say puberty is frightening.

Of course, I'm not sure. . . But I don't think this is quite what they had in mind when they came up with that saying.

I tried to focus on my breathing as the music blasted from the headphones resting snugly against my ears.

Dad had shook his head when I'd put them on and turned on my music.

"How can such noise possibly relax you?"

The standard reaction, the one that was so much like all of my friends, had come to mind immediately. . .

Parents.

It was oddly comforting to know that there was something about me that was at least a little bit normal.

Not that there's much else normal about me —especially at this point in time.

There were too many things racing around in my head at the moment—and even though I was trying *not* to think of them. . . mostly for fear that I would do something terrible without trying to. . . things just kept popping into my brain.

Like the time Mom took me to the hospital and ended up arguing with the doctor over the blood type they had listed on my form.

She had been certain he was giving her results for someone else—that somehow they had mixed up my results with someone else and didn't want to admit it.

The doctor had not understood. He'd just thought she was wrong about Dad's blood type. Looking back at it now, I was kinda glad he hadn't paid very much attention to her.

He had done the test again to make her happy, and when the results had come back the exact same way, she'd had to be content with them because, being as busy as they were, he was not about to give her any more time.

When we'd gotten home, she had gone looking for paperwork that specifically showed Dad's blood type—and then she'd done the research and found that, according to science, I shouldn't have the blood type that I had.

Fortunately, at that point, she had been concerned that her little girl could end up a lab rat somewhere and had decided to drop the whole thing.

I literally shuddered at the thought of what might have happened. If she had pushed the issue. . . and a scientist somewhere had taken interest in it. . . and he had gone looking for an explanation.

I could have ended up more than just a lab rat.

Thoughts of what could have happened started racing through my mind then; worst case scenario-type thoughts where I was taken away from Mom and locked up in some little room and experimented on daily.

Or worse. . .

When the table beside me started shaking, I moved, walking out onto the balcony to stare at the ocean.

The ocean had always been a source of peace and calm for me—and I was relieved to see that it was now as well.

I certainly did not want to attract the wrong sort of attention here. . . with my alien father in the next room.

Well, not exactly. . .

It was the human Dad in the next room—in some sort of hibernation mode.

And I was exceedingly grateful that Alien Dad had laid down on the bed, in the suite's larger bedroom, before doing whatever it was that he did when he put Human Dad into hibernation.

It was weird enough thinking about the two parts of my Dad; one Human, one Alien.

It was way too freaky to think about the fact that an alien had taken possession of the human body, and let go of that possession only part way so that he could check something on his ship—the ship that was currently parked on our moon.

You have to wonder if NASA ever notices something weird on the moon. . . something they can't explain?

That would certainly be an interesting conversation to hear.

"Sir, we don't know how to explain it."

"Well, you're going to have to figure out a way. And I want to know how long it's been there and why we didn't know about it until now."

And in my head I could see a crazy flurry of papers and people tripping over each other as they rushed off to find out how an alien spaceship had parked itself on our moon. . . and no one had noticed.

I jumped, nearly knocking my headphones to

the floor, when a bright light came from the general area of the bedroom.

What was that! I waited, but there was nothing else—and Dad did not walk into the main room.

It didn't do that when he left, did it? Had I missed it somehow?

I stayed right where I was. . . just waiting, my breath coming a little faster now, and I slipped the headphones slowly off my head. I wanted to be sure I could hear everything going on in the other room.

There was no sound—and no more lights—for several minutes, and I was just about to get up and go check it out. I didn't know what I was going to see, but I was almost terrified to not know what was happening in the other room— when Dad walked through the door holding a very odd-looking box.

"I had everything I needed on board, though I haven't looked at these things in years. . . since you were a baby." He was speaking, but it was more like he was talking to himself rather than me.

I turned my attention to the box in his hands. It was obviously made of some sort of metal, but it was like nothing I had ever seen before.

There was something odd about it. It almost looked like liquid, appearing to flow against his hands as he carried it—and the closer he got to me, the more obvious the effect was.

"I put all of this together before you were born." He set it down gently on a table that took up most of the dining area of the suite. "When it became obvious I would not need it. . ." He looked over at me with a smile. "Well, it has been in storage all this time. And now I'm glad I left it there. . . since it is needed."

I watched as he touched the top of it and the lid sort of melted away to reveal what looked like books. When he started pulling them out, I could see several odd-looking devices underneath.

I wanted to ask about them, but at the same time I was afraid to ask—not because I had any problem with reading on vacation, but because somehow the idea of asking about the books made it all the more real.

And that scared me right down to my bones.

"These will teach you." He set the books in one small stack and then pulled out one of the devices. Taking my hand, he placed the device on my palm.

It was such a tiny thing, it fit snug in my palm with room to spare all around it. It looked very similar to a rock, but I was pretty certain, without asking, that it wasn't just a rock.

"This will help you." I watched as he turned a small dial on the side—something I had not seen before—and suddenly I marveled at the strange and overwhelming calm I suddenly felt.

"Is this little thing somehow doing that?"

He was already nodding before he answered.

"It is. It will help you whenever you become overwhelmed. All you need do is set the dial to where it works best for you.

"Why does it look like a rock?"

Fancy Alien Device or Pet Rock?

He laughed before answering. "It is made to look like a small stone as a way to camouflage." He pulled a small rock from his own pocket and held it out to me. "Humans do not question this." Looking down at it with another laugh, he added, "They would question what it looks like on the home world."

He slipped it back into his pocket.

"Wait. Do you carry that with you all the time?"

He nodded.

"But you're not young. You should have control of your abilities. . . shouldn't you?" I asked the question, not entirely sure I wanted to hear the answer.

What if I never get control of these crazy abilities? What if I make something bad happen? What if I hurt someone?

"It is true that I have had control over my abilities for some time, but remember what I told you about our people. We are sometimes impulsive, acting too much on instinct. We have none of what you call common sense, just reactions—both good. . . and bad."

Again, I felt the two warring forces within me, only this time, one of them was calm and the other was fear; the bone-chilling fear that something was going to happen that I couldn't control—and I would end up losing everything.

I closed my eyes and tried to hold on to the calm—and when that didn't work, I pictured it as an ocean, and I pictured myself wading into it, letting the cool water crash over me in waves of calm.

The fear didn't stop, and it didn't go away, but it did stop controlling me. I pictured it like the sand beneath my feet.

It was there, it wasn't going anywhere, and it was still very much a force against the ocean, but. . . the ocean of calm was stronger.

When I opened my eyes, Dad was staring at me with what could only have been shock.

"How did you do that?" His voice was filled with something like awe.

"Do what?" What had I done? Was it something bad?

"You took control. And you did it without the stone."

I looked down at the small rock—or stone, as my dad called it—in my hand. I thought the thing was supposed to help me do exactly what I'd just done.

Wasn't that why he'd given it to me?

"Did I?"

"You did." He was shaking his head—and I worried for a moment that I had done something wrong, but there was nothing negative in his expression. . . only surprise.

I looked down at the stone again, wondering if it was working and maybe he didn't know it.

Maybe I don't have as much to worry about as I thought I did—if I can calm myself down without the stone. . .

"So why do you carry a rock—or stone? You didn't really answer me before."

He looked down at the ground then, and I was surprised to see a hint of red right at the tips of his ears.

Is he blushing? I didn't even know what to think about my father blushing.

He turned away before answering, and when he did, his words sounded in my head. *"It is these human emotions."* Apparently it was weird for him, too.

"They're too much sometimes?" I said it gently, not even bothering to make it a question. I knew that was what he meant.

Emotions were definitely too much too handle at times. And for someone who had not been born with them, someone who was not used to how intense or sudden they could be—or could change —I could well imagine.

"Sometimes." He answered so quietly I barely heard him.

He didn't say anything else, and I stood there, feeling pretty uncomfortable for what felt like an eternity, but was probably just a minute or two, waiting for him to say something else—anything else, but he never did.

Knowing he wasn't feeling comfortable talking about it either, I decided to drop it for now. "So, I'm supposed to keep this with me all the time?"

He cleared his throat and turned to look at me. "Yes. If your mother asks, tell her it's a pet rock. That's what she called mine. . ." He trailed off a little, and I figured it was thinking about Mom that was giving him a hard time.

I wondered if it was the emotions that had to

do with her, too. . . that made him need the small stone. Not that I was going to ask him.

Instead I focused on the stone.

"So, a pet rock. Didn't those go out of fashion like fifty years ago."

He laughed then. . . and it looked as if he was as surprised by the sound of it as I was.

"Yes. That's what your mother said, too." He rubbed a thumb over the smooth stone in his hand—and I saw it then. It glowed a little. . . just for a split second. Then I watched as his body and his face visibly relaxed.

So that's how it works. . . Impressive.

"Isn't it, though?"

I was very proud of myself for only jumping a little this time when his voice sounded in my head so unexpectedly.

I wasn't sure I would ever get used to that.

"Are you doing that on purpose or is it more of an instinct?"

"A little of both." He spoke aloud first. Then in my head again. *"Everyone on the home world communicates this way."*

"Everybody?"

He shrugged before answering. *"It is our way."*

I watched him for a moment, thinking over the idea of communicating that way.

It was strange to think about how this was just one more thing I had not known about all this time. *All these years. . . it's almost as if I've been living a lie.*

Still. . . it was an intriguing way to communicate. So, even though it felt very weird, I decided to at least give it a try. *"Why?"* And it was much easier than I had expected, almost more natural than speaking out loud.

Almost. . .

He smiled and answered immediately. *"There are a lot of reasons. The most basic is simply because that is what everyone does. You must admit, it is convenient."*

I nodded, but spoke out loud again. "Yes, but it's weird if you're not used to it."

He nodded then. "As speaking aloud was for me when I first arrived."

"I hadn't thought of that." He was nodding, but I went on quickly. "Why did you come here. . . I mean, in the beginning—before you met Mom?"

"It was an assignment." He shrugged as he answered, as if that was just a typical day for him.

I could see the to-do list in my head.

1) *Visit alien planet. . . check.*

2) Research alien beings. . . check.

3) Fall in love with alien woman. . . check.

4) Produce hybrid offspring. . . check?

"It was not quite that way."

I gasped out loud—at the same time I answered him in my mind. . . without really even meaning to. *"Okay. Now, this would be one of the times it's not exactly convenient to have someone listening in on my thoughts."*

"You make an excellent point, sweet pea."

Despite my irritation over his hearing my thoughts, I smiled when he used his pet name for me."I know I do. It is definitely not convenient for someone else to listen in on my conversations, especially when they may not realize I was only joking.

"Yes, I can see where that would be a

difficulty. . . and somewhat annoying." He laughed as his words sounded in my head.

Wanting to get back to our previous discussion—one that I was really interested in his answers, I dove back in."So, what was it like, then? Help me understand."

When he looked like he might argue, I pressed. "Because I've got to tell you, I'm really having a rough time with all of this. If just one thing could make sense, maybe it would help."

"It's not that I don't want to tell you, but that I'm not certain I can make you understand." He started in my head, but then spoke out loud. "I'm not entirely certain I understand it myself." He looked at me for a long moment before going on.

"To be perfectly truthful, there is no explanation that I can think of—at least, not one that makes sense. I had no emotion before coming here to complete my assignment." He paced back and forth in front of me, then stopped to look at me again.

"We have already established that the feelings of attachment and affection do not come from the human." He shrugged and suddenly I saw the difficulty. Finally I understood.

He had been an adult on his world. He had been used to his culture, his lack of emotion, who he was among his people. . . but when he had come here, he had been thrust into a body he was completely unfamiliar with.

Wow! That would have been a crazy adjustment to make.

"I just realized something."

"What?" He asked, when I did not immediately go on.

"Well, when you took over the human body,

everything was new to you, right?"

He didn't speak, only nodding slowly. . . carefully.

"Well, essentially that means you were kind of like a teenager." He started to speak, but I rushed on. "What I mean is, you had your adult feelings, but you were in a body that was completely foreign to you, learning everything for the first time."

10

They Say No Man is an island.

Does that count for aliens too?

"Are you saying that how I felt is how it feels to be a teenager?"

"Oh, yeah." I answered with a laugh. "And I'm not even talking about all of this new stuff going on. I mean, I can't say for absolutely certain that everything I've been going through is human stuff. . . or alien stuff, but I've had friends who've been going through puberty for over a year now."

"Puberty. . . ah. Yes. I have read about that."

I laughed again. "Yeah, I'm not sure reading about it can really do the whole thing justice. I mean, I know there's all this other stuff going on that I didn't know about. . ."

"The *alien* stuff?"

"Yeah, that. But, I mean, my body has started changing slowly over the last couple of months and I know some of it has to be human stuff, too, because it's so much like what my friends are going through."

"Ah."

"Anyway, what I was getting at is that teenagers start having all these adult kind of feelings and thoughts, but they're in this body that is still so much like a kid. It's just all sorts of weird."

"Yes, I can see where that would explain much of what I dealt with in my initial acclimation."

"It would also explain maybe how the emotions. . . the human emotions, I mean, affected you. . . the real you. . . the alien you."

"So, you are saying that because I share this body, I share the emotions within it, but perhaps it is how the emotions affect me that accounts for my feelings about your mother. . . and you."

"Exactly." He walked away from me again, and his body language was not particularly comforting.

I thought he would be happy. Didn't I just figure out the whole problem?

"That does not make the situation any better though, Zoe."

"What do you mean?" I frowned. "I mean, it

might not help, but at least it explains it. . . right?"

He sighed deeply before answering. "Yes, but I had as much as come to realize some of that already."

I started to ask what he meant, but he went on.

"When I am not here, when I am on my ship, even when I am on other assignments, I find myself thinking of you and your mother."

A warmth spread through me at the thought. Even though he had already said he cared more for me than the human part of my father did. . . or rather didn't, this was the first mention of his feeling something for us when he wasn't directly affected by the human emotions by way of being in the human body.

"Do not look like that, Zoe. This is not a

good thing."

Those words sent a chill through me. . . or was it the chaotic thoughts in his head that were affecting me?

There were no concrete thoughts coming from him that I could grab hold of, but a mess of fear and worry and images that flashed by too quickly to see anything more than what looked like my worst nightmares.

"Why isn't it a good thing? It sounds like a good thing to me. I mean, as your daughter, it certainly feels wonderful to know that you think about me when we're separated. It even answers one of the questions I've been asking myself since you started this whole thing."

"No, it is against every rule we have about exploration. . . wait, what question?"

Heat filled my cheeks. I hadn't actually meant

to say that—and now I was caught.

"Well, we have established that it was not the human part of you that made you love Mom. We have also established that it is not the human part of you that cares for me. . ."

"Loves you, Zoe." He pulled me into a hug then, holding me close for the first time in years.

"I love you more than I can understand, so much that it frightens me at times. You and your mother are my world, sweet pea."

I meant to go on, but the words escaped me. . . even in my mind. The breath hitched in my throat, closing off any hope for words as the unexpected tears escaped and slipped silently down my cheeks.

He didn't say anything, but something in the way he held me even closer made me think maybe. . . just maybe he knew I was crying.

I burrowed closer, bunching up his shirt in my fingers to hold on to him even tighter.

We stood there for a long time, holding onto each other. . . neither speaking, neither moving apart, just holding tightly to each other—as if we had been separated all this time and had just found each other. . . which was sort of the truth. . . if you really thought about it.

When he finally eased back a little, he slowly leaned away. He didn't pry my fingers from his shirt or even unwind his arms from around me. He just loosened his grip a little.

"I really do love you, baby girl. I always have, though I did not always realize that what I was feeling was love." And for some reason, the fact that he was speaking, out loud, made his words mean so much more to me.

I nodded, still unwilling to speak, mostly for

fear that I would start blubbering.

"Do you forgive me for staying away so much?"

"Of course I do, Daddy." I responded silently without even thinking. I was grateful when I realized that I could speak my thoughts in my head without fear of blubbering.

"I was just thinking how wonderful it is to hear you say that you're thinking about me when you're not with me. . . especially considering how long I have felt that you didn't really care for me at all."

"But—"

I reached up and put one finger up between us. *"But that was before I knew about all of this. I could never understand why it felt like we got along so well sometimes. . . and then other times it felt like you couldn't stand me."*

"Zoe,"

"No, I understand now, but you have to admit, it makes sense that I would be confused."

He nodded and I went on.

"I mean, how could I possibly understand— not knowing the truth?"

He shook his head as he thought the answer to me. *"Of course you would be. I am so sorry, sweetheart. I never even thought of how it would affect you."*

He leaned forward, resting his forehead against mine. *"I am beginning to understand what you meant when you said I am like a teenager."*

I laughed and he joined in a second later.

"Looks like we're in the same boat then."

"We are in good company."

* * *

Sleep was not easy to find that night.

Every time I closed my eyes I kept seeing weird mashups of the worst and most disgusting aliens I had ever seen on television and in movies.

It made perfect sense that I would be plagued with nightmares, after learning that I was part alien. . . and my dad was half alien.

I mean, what else could I expect.

Last night, even though I had asked him. . . several times. . . Dad had consistently refused to show me any pictures of what he looked like in his alien form.

I suppose I should be grateful that I don't have antennae growing out of my head and that it's my hair, instead of my skin, that's blue.

I lay in the ridiculously soft bed, while thoughts of school. . . and growing up. . . raced through my mind.

I thought about every time I had run into trouble in school. . . because I was different. . . because I was weird.

Boy, if only they knew. . . wouldn't they be surprised?

So. . . do Aliens Count Sheep, Too?

The next morning, I was a little miffed to see that I was the only one who exhibited any signs of a rough night.

Maybe even more than a little.

When Dad said "Good Morning." I grunted in response.

When he asked me how I had slept, I tried to glare, but I was just too tired.

For some reason, he was in a ridiculously cheery mood. So much so that I almost. . . almost. . . wondered if I had somehow dreamed yesterday or imagined it all.

And then my coffee mug shook, just a little, when I reached for it. . . almost like it was trying to come to my hand.

I snatched my hand back and looked up at him when I heard the sigh he must have let out.

"I thought we might get out on the beach today." He gestured to the window—and the sun streaming in. "After all, we are on vacation, aren't we? Let's go walk in the surf."

I ignored him and reached for my cup again, ignoring the tremor that stopped only when I took a firm grip on it.

"Perhaps we just need a distraction."

Squinting against the brightness of the room,

the early hour, and the complete lack of any decent sleep, I poured coffee into my cup, added creamer and then sipped recklessly, long before it was cool enough to drink.

"I know this is likely a bad time to ask, but does your mother really allow you to drink coffee?" When I turned to glare at him, he added, "Isn't thirteen kind of young to want—or need—coffee?"

"For your information, I've been drinking coffee for years." I bit back the slightly rude retort that came to mind about how would he know I was too young to be drinking coffee. I also reminded myself that he might not be able to help being one of those mercilessly cheerful morning people.

"Oh." was his only response.

I continued to drink my coffee, waiting for

the caffeine to hit my system and wake the brain cells that had finally managed to succumb to sleep during my restless night.

He stood at the window, drinking his own coffee, looking over at me, then out the window. . . and then back to me.

"Does the beach sound good to you?"

"Honestly, sleep sounds good to me right now."

"Did you not sleep well?" His voice held a note of concern.

I looked at him with half-closed eyes, my voice nearly a snarl. "I barely slept at all."

When he said nothing else, I went back to drinking my coffee. I was finally starting to feel the effects of the caffeine. At least I felt a bit more alert.

"Why are you so chipper?" I held up a hand

before he could answer. "No, wait. I'm guessing you slept just fine." Under my breath, I added, "Probably some alien thing."

Just as he answered."I do not sleep."

"You don't. . . Wait, you don't sleep? Ever? You don't need to sleep? Seriously?"

"Seriously? Yes, I am serious." His voice had a note of confusion that told me he wasn't sure why I was asking or why it seemed like a big deal to me.

"Aw, man. Why couldn't I have gotten that ability? I waste so much time sleeping. And trying to wake up is even worse—especially after a rough night."

"It is quite logical that your human side would require some of the things that are necessary for humans. Sleep must be one of them."

"Wait, but if you don't sleep, what do you do? Did you keep the poor human shell up all night too?" I was surprised to realize that I actually felt bad for the man who didn't like me. . . had never liked me, but nonetheless I felt sorry for him.

Especially if he feels anything at all like I do right now. Though that made no sense. If the human part of him felt this way, he couldn't be in such a good mood.

"The human slept. I was on my ship."

"Oh. That makes sense—I guess." Though I had no idea how he accomplished that feat. So I went back to my coffee. I would need to be more awake to deal with the confusion.

*   *   *

Long before I was really awake enough to

deal with other people, Dad finally convinced me to get out on the beach.

Dragged is more like it. I thought acidly. . . half-hoping he was listening in at the moment.

Though his behavior showed no signs that he was listening to the acidic comments that were running through my mind the entire time I was getting changed into the swimsuit I still wasn't certain I liked, or as I trudged behind him as he headed down to the beach.

He was convinced the distraction was just what I needed to help me deal with everything I had learned in the last twenty-odd hours.

*   *   *

Once we were down on the beach, I could feel the tension that had been my constant companion over the last few days start to drain away, and though I was reluctant to admit that he was somewhat right, I was glad I had come down with him.

The sand, the sun, and the beautiful ocean was just what I needed after the hectic flight, plus a crazy day, and rough night.

I jumped waves for a long time with Dad, until he decided he was going farther out than I was comfortable with. For a while, I jumped by myself. Then, when I tired of the constant splash, I retreated to shallower water and watched him from a distance for a time.

Then I decided to walk down the beach and back in the surf, hunting for shells and people watching.

And when I tired of that, I snuggled up with a book in one of the fancy lounge chairs the hotel provided in a nice shady area while Dad paddled out and waited for waves that were big enough for him to surf.

I would never have imagined he would be a surfer. Surfers are so cool. . . and he's. . . well, he's pretty cool, even if he's my dad.

But knowing what I now knew about who my father really was, he wasn't someone I would have expected to see paddling out to sea on a surfboard like some teenager with long hair and a crazy dark tan—or a bunch of tattoos.

The image made me laugh and I realized that I had no idea how old Alien Dad actually was. I had assumed he was an adult because it made sense to me, but there really was no way to know if he had been an adult or not on his own world. He could have been a wet-behind-the-ears newbie who got stuck with the crap assignment no one else wanted.

That idea had me laughing again. It was several minutes before I went back to reading my book.

Eventually, he decided he'd had enough sun or the waves were beginning to disappoint, because he showed up next to me, wet and grinning widely.

"Are you hungry?"

And I realized I was. "Yeah."

"Let's go eat, then." He was still grinning and his obvious enthusiasm—coupled with my own great day—was infectious and I found myself grinning right back at him.

All the way back to the room he chatted about the waves and the water. He laughed and asked me about my walk, whether I had found any good shells, and if I had enjoyed my book.

I happily answered each question, thinking all the while that this might actually turn into a pretty great vacation after all.

Wait! Don't Count Those Eggs Yet.

You know what they say about. . . counting your chickens before they hatch. . .

There should really be a saying like that for vacation moments, too. *Something along the line of the other shoe dropping. . .*

We ate in the hotel dining room, which made me nervous.

On the beach, in an environment that was

very soothing to me, I had felt comfortable, not worried at all about the new abilities I still had very little control over.

Honestly, I had almost forgotten about them at times.

Inside, sitting in an unfamiliar and somewhat fancy surrounding, I felt much too exposed. I was actually tempted to just sit on my hands, though I wasn't really sure that would do any good. This time I was glad that Dad had been listening in on my thoughts. His words in my head took me completely by surprise—it was all I could do not to gasp. *"You have your stone with you, yes?"*

"Yes." I briefly wondered if he could hear the mental hiss that I was imagining going along with the word in my mind—as I glared at him beside me.

He was not the least bit deterred. *"It will*

help, Zoe. I promise. You should always carry it with you."

"I am carrying it." I wondered if there was a mental image of my gritted teeth to go along with the mental tone I hoped he could hear. . . or see. . . however it worked.

He showed no sign of a tone or imagery influencing him one bit. *"I do not understand why you are so opposed to the stone. . . especially since it will help you control your new abilities around people."*

"Could we not do this here?" When he looked at me over his water glass with an incredulous expression, I added, *"Please."*

He shook his head, but stopped, turning his attention to the menu.

"So, what looks good?"

I rolled my eyes at his theatrics, though it was

somewhat reassuring to see that he could imitate a human so well.

He went on like that for the entire meal. He made a production of ordering. He kept up a steady stream of small talk while we ate. He even insisted we order desert.

The trouble really started when we headed back to the room.

"So, you are going to explain all of this to Mom, aren't you?

"That would be a very bad idea."

He held up a finger as I started to speak. *"Okay. Fine. Why would it be a bad idea to tell Mom about all of this?"*

"It would not be safe for her."

When other people came out of the hotel restaurant behind us, we moved toward the elevators.

"You do know she's going to notice when I freak out and start moving things around the room. . . right?"

He said. . . and thought. . . nothing, so I pressed on.

"How am I supposed to explain that?" I jabbed the button for the elevator. . . hard.

"You will have control before I send you back home."

I huffed out a breath as we moved into the elevator that had just opened. *"You can't know that. I may never get control."*

He turned to look at me, gripping my shoulders in his hands—not so much that it hurt, but tightly. And I was glad we were the only ones in the elevator. His expression was so intense, it was like I could feel it in my bones.

"Zoe, you will find control. You must. This is

essential. You do not want to draw the attention of my superiors. It could be bad for more than just you if that were to happen."

"What do you mean?"

"You do not wish to know."

I started to speak again, but he squeezed my shoulders and motioned slightly with his head.

I looked up at the corner of the elevator. It took me a few seconds to spot the small camera that was discreetly positioned, but I got the message and did not say anything else.

"When we are in the room."

I looked up at him, worried now. *"How do you know there aren't cameras in there too?"*

"I scanned the rooms before we checked in. There are no cameras in any of them. The room is safe as long as we are not loud enough for anyone on either side to hear."

I said nothing else out loud, but my thoughts were a mess of chaos. They jumped from how unfair it was that I couldn't tell Mom about any of this. . . to how crazy it was to think that some alien way off out in space might decide to come here and do. . . something to me or Dad or even Mom, if I didn't get control or slipped up and told someone.

*   *   *

Who do they think they are anyway!

We had barely made it through the door to the room when my control snapped, letting loose a crazed whirlwind that swirled around me in a frenzied pattern of twists and gusts.

It was so thick, I couldn't see clearly through it. Everything was completely blurred and all I could see was the ends of my short hair whipping around on either side of my face.

I tried breathing. I tried squeezing the stupid stone that was supposed to help. I imagined myself back on the beach, with the ocean flowing in at my feet, swallowing up the fear and anger that was threatening to consume me.

And then somehow Dad reached through the dizzying winds and found my hands. He took hold of both of them—and the calm within him somehow started to seep into me.

The wind slowed.

My vision cleared.

I took a deep breath. And then another until I finally started to feel settled.

And I knew I should calm down more before I asked, but the questions would not stay silent.

"So. . . what about me? What exactly will they do if they find out about me?" The terrifying possibilities sent a chill down my spine.

What would they do? *What could they do—to me and to Dad? Maybe even to Mom?*

He pulled me close then. *"I will never let anyone hurt you, Zoe. You have to believe me. I am sorry. I did not intend to give you the impression that they would do something to you."*

"But what would they do if they found out."

I could feel the panic growing, and it did not help one bit that he didn't answer my question completely.

"We are not going to tell them—and they have no jurisdiction on Earth. They would not dare do anything to interfere."

I knew he was trying to reassure me now, but nothing he was saying made me feel any better.

"But they would have some jurisdiction over me, wouldn't they? I'm one of them. . . or at least

half of me is."

"But half of you is human. And your mother is completely human. They would not dare to harm you or her. It goes against the most basic laws about who we are as a people."

"But they can do something to you. And they could take you away, couldn't—" My voice broke before I could finish.

His arms tightened around me again. And he tucked my head under his chin, enveloping me, not just in the safety of his arms, but in the warmth of his heart. . . and the calm that was flowing from him. . . into me.

Though it did not make the fear go away. It just buried it under a mountain of calm.

Gifts I Would Really Like to Return

It's one thing to fall out of bed. . .

It's quite another to wake up floating. . . levitating several feet above the bed you're supposed to be sleeping in, especially when you weren't sleeping all that well to begin with.

With no warning—and no real intention of my own—I dropped! I landed on the bed with an "umph", that pushed out all the air in my lungs.

I lay there for what seemed like a long time, just looking up at the ceiling, watching the shadows that danced across the white that was more gray in the dark room.

How he thought I would be able to just drop right off to sleep, I will never know. Not with all of this stuff in my head.

Especially not knowing that something could happen to my father—at least the one who actually liked me.

There were dozens of questions running around in my mind. . . like why this had never happened before. Really, had no other scout they'd sent to a planet become so enamored with the people of that world that they had become involved and then romantically linked?

And if they hadn't, had they really learned anything about the planet—or its people? Was it really possible to only observe and actually learn anything?

Was it just humans who were so emotional, susceptible to such attraction. . . and connection? That didn't feel possible.

There had to be other beings out there like us. . . didn't there?

I nearly laughed aloud at the one-sided conversation going on in my head. Was I really arguing that there had to be other aliens out in the universe that were just like humans?

Three days ago, I didn't even know there were people—or aliens—on other planets. And now I'm arguing. . . with myself. . . over whether or not any of them are like humans.

I must be losing my mind.

For some reason, that brought the other problem—the more serious problem—to mind.

For whatever reason, Dad had done something he shouldn't have.

And if his bosses somehow found out, he would be in trouble.

At worst. . . I stopped myself before I let that thought have too much room in my head. I didn't want to think about what could happen. It was bad enough knowing that something could happen.

And since a lot of it hangs on whether or not I can figure out how to control all these crazy new abilities, I need to stop stressing.

Unable to shut my brain off and knowing that I would just go back to a bad place if I didn't distract myself, I rolled towards the edge of the bed and slid my feet into the fuzzy slippers I'd brought from home.

They were unnecessary, but they were

comforting and they made me feel less awkward padding around the enormous room. Picking up my cellphone and checking automatically for texts from Mom, I walked over to the desk that sat by a large window with a view of the ocean.

There were no new texts and I was in no mood to deal with any of the drama on social media, so I set the phone down, clicked on the small desk lamp, and picked up the strange books Dad had pulled from the same box he had pulled the calming stone from.

So, these are supposed to teach me about who I am. . . what I am. . .

When I picked up the first one, all I saw at first were symbols that made no sense to me at all.While I stared at it, trying to decipher what they could possibly mean, the symbols changed—right before my eyes.

I dropped the book with a heavy clank of the metallic cover.

Yikes!

When I had my nerve up I reached for it again. . . and once again, the symbols were unreadable until I concentrated on them. Once they changed, I could read them.

Training guide: how to take control of your powers, and keep them from controlling you.

Someone has a wicked sense of humor.

Still, it was odd thinking that there were actually aliens on their world who needed help with learning to control their powers.

At least I'm not alone in it. I would need to ask Dad in the morning if they went through some sort of puberty. Maybe that was when they had difficulty controlling their abilities.

Or maybe it's some sort of rite-of-passage

ceremony, where they get their full abilities and then they have to learn how to control them at full throttle.

The idea made me feel somewhat better. My difficulty was not because I was part human or because I had only just gotten my abilities.

This was something the aliens on his world went through—enough that they needed a manual to help them out.

Gosh, I'm glad he thought to get it for me.

I read for hours, slowly turning the pages and looking over the words that read like one of the dummy books Mom had for figuring out how to do things around the house that she said would be silly to call a repairman for.

The more I read, the quicker the alien symbols translated, though there was very little that actually helped me. . . just lots of suggestions about avoiding stressful things and about using the calming stone.

And Dad hadn't been kidding. The picture in the book obviously did not translate and it looked nothing at all like the smooth stone that was sitting on my little bedside table.

It looked like a complex machine, metal and shiny, with lights all over.

It doesn't even look like any of the machines we have here. No wonder they camouflaged Dad's and made it look like a rock.

I picked up the other device that Dad had given me. It looked like a rock as well, but it was much larger than the calming stone, which was comforting because it meant there was no way I could get the two mixed up.

It was also an entirely different color, a much darker grey. . . almost black, and had a metallic sheen to it. If anyone looked at it for very long, they could conceivably question whether or not it was actually a rock.

Which is probably why he made a point of telling me to keep it hidden. Which made sense anyway when I thought about it. I certainly wouldn't want anyone to take it.

I finished the first book and started on the second, which turned out to be a history of the planet and the people that were at least partly mine.

I suppressed a groan. *Isn't it enough I have to read about human history? Now I have to learn about theirs, too.* Though I reminded myself that it was mine too—at least a little bit.

Knowing my track record with history, coupled with the late hour, I picked up the book and my phone and went back to bed, crawling between the covers and snuggling up with the book propped up on my legs.

EPILOGUE

What Are You Doing Here?

The voice that woke me the next morning was far away, as if someone were calling me from the beach.

"Zoe?"

There was quiet and then my name again, more insistent this time. *"Zoe! You have to wake up."*

I sat straight up in bed, throwing the covers off and rushing out of the bedroom.

The man sitting at the dining table was not the Dad who liked me.

He looked up when I skidded to a halt in the

main room, ground his teeth together—*probably at the sight of my stupid hair*—then looked back down at the newspaper in his hand.

I turned and ran back into my bedroom.

The other odd device Dad had given me was flashing red and orange. I hurried over to the desk and picked it up, but I had no idea how to use it.

An odd blue light appeared on the bottom and after a second, it beeped and then a hologram appeared.

The face I was looking at was decidedly not human, the features elongated and a very odd shade of green, certainly not one found anywhere on Earth. I nearly dropped the thing in surprise, but suddenly my dad's voice—the dad who loved me—sounded in my head. . . familiar, though a bit panicked.

"Zoe, please do not be angry with me. I

cannot help going this time. I have been recalled without warning. I was barely able to bring the human out of hibernation before they pulled me back."

Since I wasn't certain the communicator could even pick up my voice, I answered the same way he had spoken.

"Wait. . . what? They pulled you back? Are you already there? Are you not on your ship? What's wrong? What happened? When will you be back?"

Even my thoughts were an incoherent mess by this point. All of the fears I had been trying to suppress were filling my chest, choking me.

"Zoe, I do not want you to worry. I will come back—one way or another. I will not leave you."

"But how can you. . ."

He cut me off. *"I must go, sweet pea. I am*

getting close enough that they will pick up my thoughts."

A phantom feather-light kiss brushed my cheek as he went on. *"Read your books. Use the stone. Contact me only in the most dire emergency. Be cautious."*

As the first tear escaped my eyes, he added, *"I love you."*

The image blinked away and I was left feeling more empty than ever. He was gone and I had no way of knowing when. . . or if. . . he would be back.

No matter what he said, if they could take him away so easily, he might not have any choice but to stay—and never return.

I dropped down onto the floor. . . too devastated to even cry.

THE END. . .

For now.

"Have I not commanded you? Be strong and courageous. Do not be afraid; for the LORD your GOD will be with you wherever you go."

~ Joshua 1:9

A NOTE FROM JC

It is a difficult thing; to be a young girl who has a miserable relationship with her father. This story was born in part from memories of my own difficult relationship with my father.

That I went through life feeling as if I was a step out of sync with everyone around me had a significant impact on it as well. It's difficult to grow up feeling as if you don't fit anywhere.

Many times I have felt like an alien even in my own skin. Fortunately, God has had a plan for my life all along and I finally feel as if I am in it.

~ JC

"Call unto me, and I will answer thee,
and shew thee great and mighty things,
which thou knowest not."
~ Jeremiah 33:3

ABOUT THE AUTHORS

JC Morrows is an author of fantastical fiction filled with faith. She writes about assassins, aliens, dragons, angels, fairy tales, and teenagers trying desperately to survive in post-apocalptic worlds. She also drinks coffee. . . lots and lots of coffee.

Macy Morrows is a young girl following in her mother's footsteps, with storytelling, having her head in the clouds, and spending her time in fictional worlds. She fits in better than her mother ever did though. . . and that's not a bad thing.

A NOTE FROM MACY

When Mom asked me to help her write this story, I have to admit the first thing I got really excited about was dressing up like Zoe for author events.

As Mom wrote more of the story, I started to feel like Zoe and I were friends and her story has become very important to me. I'm thrilled to be a part of telling it.

I am looking forward to meeting readers and other young writers, sharing Zoe's story with them, and encouraging them to be true to who they are, no matter what.

~ Macy

"For God so loved the world, that He gave His only begotten Son, that whosoever believeth in Him should not perish, but have everlasting life."

~ John 3:16

ABOUT THE PUBLISHER

Christian Publishing for HIS GLORY

S&G Publishing offers books with messages that honor Jesus
Christ to the world! S&G works with Christian authors to
bring you the best in "inspirational" fiction
and non-fiction.

S&G is proud to publish a variety of
Christian fiction genres:
inspirational romance
young reader
young adult
speculative
historical
suspense

Check out our website at
sgpublish.com

AMISH SWEET SHOP

MYSTERIES

BY NAOMI MILLER

CPSIA information can be obtained
at www.ICGtesting.com
Printed in the USA
LVOW13s1243280318
571444LV00008B/32/P